BEHIND THE PERFECT PICTURE

DEANA-KAY THOMAS

RESTORATION OF THE BREACH
WITHOUT BORDERS

ISBN: 978-1-954755-53-6

Published by:
Restoration of the Breach without Borders
West Palm Beach, Florida 33407
restorativeauthor@gmail.com
Tele: (561) 388-2949

Cover Design aided by:
Rachel Henry

Editor:
Melisha Bartly-Ankle

Formatting and Publishing done by:
Sherene Morrison

ENDORSEMENTS

Deana-Kay Thomas has taken us behind the veil to reveal to us what she had to endure growing up as a "Purpose Child." She shares how she survived emotional, sexual, psychological, and physical abuse. This work of art is a testimony about the protective, providing, merciful, loving hand of God and confirmation of Philippians 1:6 "being confident of this very thing, that He who has begun a good work in you will complete it until the day of Jesus Christ" ... and speaks truth to the saying **"Purpose cannot die".**

> --Hillary Dunkley-Campbell
> Author
> I am Encouraged and What is Stopping You?

* * * * * *

Behind the Perfect Picture is a riveting book of a formidable young woman who defies all odds, conquers her fears, and rose above all disappointments in pursuit of her dreams. Deana-Kay Thomas has made her mark in writing such a powerful, yet piercing book permeated with live changing experiences. A definite Must Read!

--Domenique Martin,
Project Management &
Marketing Ambassador

FOREWORD

I am beyond thrilled to do the foreword for Deana-Kay

Thomas' first book, on such a dynamic and powerful topic: "Behind the perfect picture" She has yielded herself to be used by God, and indeed a daughter of purpose and blessing. I have had the privilege of knowing her mother who sought the Lord for many years for the blessing of the fruit of the womb. Jeremiah 1:5 is in full effect.

"Before I formed thee in the belly, I knew thee; and before thou camest forth out of the womb I sanctified thee, and I ordained thee a prophet unto the nations."

Deana-Kay is purposely ordained by God and I give thanks to the Holy Spirit for entrusting her with this big assignment of writing this book.

Deana-Kay is paving the way for a new and chosen generation to break out of a structure of fear into freedom and fulfillment. I have loved the times of connecting with Sis Deana-kay, one of my Scripture

Drill Students, Youth Ambassador and Worshipper. Look what the Lord has done.

This book will be an encouragement to all readers. It will help you discover your hidden purpose while going through the bruising of life. I do find this book to be riveting and captivating.

So many people have been plagued with hurts and wounds, yet they have mastered the art of concealing, wearing false smiles, that literally masked the hidden bruises. Deana-kay has brought to light that there is great wealth in exposing the scars. In Spite of the insecurities, shackles of abuse and pain that she faced, God has been faithful in doing a work of healing and restoration in her life.

In her book she shared how one can overcome adversity. No matter the attacks of the enemy it is only a part of the process towards the Lord's intent for your life.

Beyond the Perfect Picture" is authored by a beautiful, anointed and chosen Vessel of God, who chooses to walk with Him despite the trial's life throws at her.

She is now vulnerable in his presence and has not held back embracing the challenges, appreciating the struggles, and living a life consoled by God.

As you read this inspirational text, allow the Holy Spirit to minister to your every need. It is all for His Purpose and His Glory!

Yes! Get your life in God's Hands.

Remember "Behind the Perfect Picture" is not only for you.

--Min Donna Morris
Author
Moved to a New Mindset:
Free from limitations, rejections
& fears"
Marriage Mentor,
Christan Life Coach

TABLE OF CONTENTS

CHAPTER 1

DEATH

"**I** am going to die, and you and Dean are going to cry for me," were the words my mother uttered to me, a few months before her death. As I sat with her on the verandah, I understood what she was saying, and that reality made me afraid. It brought tears to my eyes that I was about to lose my mother, Juliet Thomas. She died when I was eight years old.

She was not just a mother; she was a determined soul who desired and loved God. My heroine, who risked her life to bring me into this world, was gone. How could that be? Why would someone so precious be taken from her child? I had not gotten enough time to get to know her. She had faith to believe that she had to give birth to a child before leaving the earth and that selfless action allowed me to love her even more. She is forever in my heart. I did not understand then but now things are clearer, the nights she would kneel at her bedside praying for my father and me. As she prayed, she said, "Lord, build a fence around Dean" and "Lord, give Deana-Kay a good education."

> *"Sometimes you will never know the values of a moment until it becomes a memory". --Dr. Seus.*

The mentioned quote grabbed my attention. Based on my age, I never knew how to value the time spent with my mother. I thought that I would have her forever but now I only have her memories. She ensured before her departure that she gave birth to purpose- ***I am Purpose.***

THE BEGINNING

My mother and father were high school sweethearts; it was love at first sight. However, my father's friends tried to influence him not to marry my mother because at that time she had not yet given him a child. However, despite the negativities that surrounded the relationship, they could not stop my parents from getting married. They eventually defeated the odds and brought purpose into this world. It may seem unfathomable, but God has perfect timing. Dean and Juliet went on to tie the knot; yes!! God is good.

After a blissful marriage, the couple got pregnant. After months of waiting, the long-awaited baby was on the way. My mother had complications. Diabetes had caused fertility challenges but when Jesus says it is time no other heavenly or earthly being can change that decree. My mother was a praying woman and a prophetess, always in the Spirit. Therefore, her faith in God kept her in prayer, and other folks from the church prayed as well. Like Hannah in first Samuel chapter 1, my mother maintained her focus in prayer. She prayed relentlessly until she conceived and gave birth to a bouncing baby girl who weighed 7 pounds. Yes, that is me!!, Purpose Child

After all that she had been through I became my mother's 'handbag' (we were always together). We shared a bond that was unmatched. As a little girl in church, I was told that no one got the opportunity to hold me as my mother did not believe in disturbing others' worship. Hence, she held me the entire time; only allowing me to sit on the bench when the Holy Spirit hovered over her. Yes, I was indeed her handbag.

I AM PURPOSE

There were times I felt like giving up on life and by extension committing suicide. However, when you are chosen, taking your life is not an option for you. You may attempt suicide, but it will not happen because amid the challenges only what God says about you shall prevail. As I reflect on my life's journey, I remember age thirteen when I wanted to commit suicide. I went to the refrigerator with the intention of taking Humulin

R fast acting insulin that would plunge me into a diabetic coma or even kill me after 30 minutes without eating. I had my plan well-orchestrated and was ready to take action; however, when I opened the refrigerator the insulin Humulin R fell and broke. My plan was unsuccessful and that made me understand the Lord's grace and purpose that was and is over my life.

Purpose is the reason for which something or someone exists. Deana-Kay Thomas exists for a reason. A life journey filled with uncertainty, yet she rises and shines like a diamond. Jeremiah 1:5 states "Before I formed you in the womb, I knew you; before you were born, I sanctified [a] you; I ordained you a prophet to the nations." My life seemed like a far cry from purpose but the mentioned verse gave me comfort and peace knowing that God created me for a specific purpose. Some individuals might not understand God's grace that is on my life but I do. I have come to understand the unmerited favor of God in its entirety because of how marred, broken and undone I was; but God still loved and had a place in His family for me.

5

When you are chosen by God you have, knowingly or unknowingly, signed a contract of greatness with Him. In essence, you enter a binding agreement that sees the Lord of Hosts fighting on your behalf to ensure that the obstacles to greatness are removed. In other words, you do not have any other choice but to be great. It does not matter how far you run and hide, how long you stay in a messy situation or how deep you are in sin, once God says that you are chosen then you must fulfill your part of that contract of greatness. Like Jonah from the Bible, fear may have gotten the upper hand and you are hiding in the hinder part of the ship but purpose can never hide from the Creator; even in the midst of hell He is there. This was made even clearer when people would say to me "You are a purpose 'enuh', and you are blessed," said phrase was what others would use to start a conversation, but my response was always a smile. Years after I realized that I was created for a reason and that amid life's challenges, nothing can stop me from being the woman of God that the Lord wants me to be, I gladly welcome the sentiments expressed by others.

THE COVENANT

Covenants, especially the ones that are divinely made, should not be treated with scant regard. I understand that I am a covenant child because my mother prayed for me, and I also experienced a lot of heartache. When you are a covenant child you cannot do as you please for every action has consequences. You are not like everybody else. You are *CALLED*. You are *CHOSEN.* You are *DIFFERENT,* set apart for God and His Glory.

On a particular day at church as pastor ministered about covenant through the leading of the Holy Spirit I reflected on the stories of Samson and Samuel. Both were not only Bible characters but covenant children and that confirmed to me that I am a covenant child. However, while Samuel chose to be set apart for the work that God had for him, Samson chose to go against what the Lord said and faced serious consequences. If I had chosen my path in this life by disregarding God's desire I would have died. I would have lived a purposeless life. I chose life by walking in the will of

7

the Lord. However, choosing to walk in purpose does not mean all the challenges will magically disappear. The journey is punctuated with temptations, sin, brokenness, hurt and insecurities but God is always there patiently waiting for purpose to be birthed and that makes it all worthwhile.

The truth is although I knew I was a purpose child I wanted my *WILL*. I wanted to live life my way so I chose a partner and orchestrated a plan to get this person saved and eventually we would be married. In my quest I was drawn away from God which almost cost my life. I literally felt as though I was going to die; I tasted death. I felt sick and would have countless panic attacks. The fear of dying was very strong. My feet got so cold, food became insipid and I felt like that was the end. I had countless demonic attacks as they would come for me in my sleep; sometimes I was even afraid to go to bed. Hence, I learnt that being a covenant child is not something to take for granted, you can lose your life. As a result, I do not play with the calling of God; the covenant is serious. When you are a covenant child or even a believer, you have to learn to wait on God. Being in the Will of God requires you waiting on Him because his timing is perfect. You are a purpose, so wait on the Lord and let him do the impossible, the suddenly   and the immediately in your life.

Being called for purpose is a discipline. When walking with Christ, one has to learn to kill flesh and totally denounce the things and taste of the world. The process I went through taught me how to walk holy and disciplined before the Lord. I am grateful for every experience I have gone through because they help to shape the woman I am today. I now fully understand walking in and being a covenant child.

CHAPTER 2

THE SEEMINGLY PERFECT LIFE

After the death of my mother, my father lost his job and as a result he turned to drinking and smoking. Although I had family members, I had no one to stay with but my father and he was not financially stable to help me throughout this life. Additionally, he had a mistress, and we did not get along very well. Being aware of my situation, my two aunts expressed their concerns to someone named Lady Witch who willingly offered to assist me. Thereafter, I began spending weekends and special holidays with her. She treated me well and as a result I told my father that I wanted to live with her. He agreed and I went to live with Lady Witch. At first, I thought that everything was going to be alright. I thought that I was now at a safe place where I could grow and blossom into *purpose*. I was young but I had a relationship with God. I knew Him and would talk to Him about everything.

10

I was comfortable in a huge house; the rooms were spacious and nice; I had my own. I was never hungry, for a time. I had a lot of nice things including lovely clothing, shoes and hairstyles. Additionally, I would go to exquisite places with Lady Witch, I thought that was the life, a dream life for every eleven-year-old. The introduction to the good things continued for about two years then I started experiencing the total opposite of what I was exposed to. My family living in Payne Avenue thought that I was alright because I painted a picture-perfect scenario. When I was passing, I looked beautiful on the outside but I was dying on the inside. I could not tell my family what was going on. I thought all that was happening was because I did not want to live in the inner-city. I did not see my family for a while. We became estranged as Lady Witch started telling lies that made me wanted to hate my family. (In Jamaican parlance turn my mind against my family.)

She took care of my physical needs, but I was emotionally distressed. I hated myself. I thought I was not beautiful because of the hurtful things Lady Witch would say to me.

She called me Ugly. She compared me to my mother and cursed my feet. (Yuh si how yuh foot back look like yuh mother own). Look at your feet and how they resemble those of your mother's. She would call me derogatory names such as, Bitch, Worthless and Half Dead Gal. However, I stayed because I did not want to go back to Payne Avenue to live with my family. I was so immune to the "good" or seemingly "perfect life" that I did not want to give it up. Therefore, I stayed, endured the pain, the hurt, the abuse, and the bad treatment. I vividly remember her beating me with a belt from my head to toes for no reason. I remember the hit I got in my face without any explanation. I remember the nights crying before I went to bed. I remember her relaxing my hair and while it was burning my head, she told me not to wash out the relaxer. I started crying as my scalp was badly burnt. Along with those abuses, I felt like the maid of the house, I hardly got enough rest. I could not sleep late in bed; I had to get up to do household chores.

The load was now too much to bear. The fancy clothes could not ease the pain; going to the different places could not eradicate the feelings and that was when the thoughts of suicide started to plague me. I would literally hide in different areas of the house and just weep. While cleaning the house I would be crying. I cried until I started feeling pain in my chest and throat. When I thought I no longer could manage that life, I started planning my escape strategy from the house.

I hid the pain so well that no one knew what was happening to me. I wore a smile, dressed up and showed up at school, at church and anywhere I went with Lady Witch, *Behind the Perfect Picture* indeed.

CHAPTER 3

SHACKLED BY ABUSES AND PAIN

The pain became excruciatingly unbearable. I honestly believe that no one on this earth should ever encounter such pain and agony through this life. I felt like a crushed rose left to die without purpose. The things I went through on this journey called life allowed me to wonder why I was born. Life was unfair to me, I thought. It started one morning when I was awakened from sleep as Lady Witch yelled my name saying it is time to get out of bed and wash the bathroom. I was so tired from the previous day's work.

Eventually I crawled out of bed to begin another day filled with work. I felt like a slave on a big plantation. After cleaning the bathroom, I was outside washing my undergarments; I had the pipe on with the aim of filling the sink then I heard Lady Witch shouted from the kitchen that I should turn off the pipe. 'Hey gyal lack off mi pipe or yuh si what I am going to duh yuh" (turn off the pipe or watch what I will do to you). I did not turn off the pipe at the same time then I heard Lady Witch coming towards me very angry. She threw my undergarments out of the sink into the dirt then she punched me in my stomach. On receiving that blow I knelt on the floor and cried uncontrollably.

Unfortunately, my cousin who witnessed my anguish just laughed at me to scorn as I cried. In that moment I said to myself I need to get out of this house, away from Lady Witch. As I thought about the plan the abuse continued and I was hurting more, it was just too much for one child to endure. I asked God why me continuously. It became such an anthem that I began questioning God's love for me.

Again, I was back at the chores. It was Saturday morning; I was washing my clothes on the outside and I was a little upset. Lady Witch asked me to carry a pan of water to fill another so that she could finish washing her clothes. I am not sure if I took too long to respond but Lady Witch got upset, pushed me to the floor and kicked me in my vagina. I was truly taken off guard by her action, but I knew that Lady Witch would pass remarks that she did not like me.

However, with all the abuse, I admire God's sense of care in strategically placing His people into my life. On a particular day after I recently graduated, I went to a high school function to do a speech. Upon leaving the house the Holy Spirit told me to take my resume with me. I questioned the idea, but I was obedient to the voice of God. When I arrived at the venue, I saw a lady in high gear in her floral dress and red heels, she spoke with such confidence. My speech came after hers. After the function we met outside and right there the very lady asked me for my resume and I gave it to her, things seemed as though they were turning for my good. Following that encounter she became my best friend and spiritual mother. She prayed for me and that is when all hell broke loose at home... Things were already very terrible and meeting this wonderful woman of God made it worse. However, the divine connection was for my own development and preparation for the task ahead. Although I was now hopeful, the abuses continued. For no apparent reason

Lady Witch continuously yelled "I don't like you; God take her out of my life, me nuh like her "I do not like her. I was told to wash the dishes and when the task was not done in the specified time, Lady Witch would use a belt and or anything that she grabbed even a big iron spoon or fork to beat me.

During one of the many crazy seasons I endured with Lady Witch, there was no water in the community but there were some drums in the yard that needed filling. I remember very clearly that my cousins, who were now living with Lady Witch, and I had to carry the huge yellow canola oil bottles filled with water across the Tarrant playing field through the neighbor's backyard and then to the house I was staying, that was repeated multiple times until the drums were filled. What was even worse we could not use the water we carried to do anything at all. That along with everything else left me feeling like a maid. I had to wash everybody's clothes including their underwear, clean rooms, iron curtains and decorate rooms for guests. I was tired most of the time.

I was even asked to care for the baby of a friend who was visiting from abroad; I was in ninth grade at the time. I had to bathe and give the baby all that was needed before I went to school. One night I remember being awoken by some slaps and Lady Witch yelling" a kill yuh want to kill the woman pickney" "are you going to kill the woman's child?" The baby was crying but I was so tired I became confused and gave her the stale milk instead of making a fresh bottle.

BEATEN IN THE HEAD WITH A BELT

I cannot recall what led to the incident, but I remember being beaten in the head with a belt until a clip that was holding my hair broke. As was said I cannot explain but I was getting so many blows to the head that one of my cousins had to try and take what Lady Witch had in her hand. On another occasion I was told to do something, I was in the process of completing the task when I was approached and beaten with a belt all over my body. The belt buckle hit me in my eye which made it

18

discolored, black, and blue. I was so embarrassed that when I went to school, I told them I fell.

THINGS TOOK A TURN FOR THE WORSE

I was in my last year of high school and things got even worse. I had to walk to school and waited every day for the PATH lunch because I had no money. I was not getting food at home but again God was watching over purpose. He provided The Programme of Advancement Through Health and Education (PATH) so that I could be given a warm lunch daily. Eventually, I graduated from high school after which I got a job working as an apprentice at my alma mater. I can truly say the enemy had a plan for my life but God, even before I was born, did not just have a plan but He intentionally carved out a purpose for my life.

Note that while we walk in God's plan the enemy will present himself, sometimes even in disguise. I met this man who was like a friend to me at first. The same day we met he asked me to come and see him later that night. My cousin and I went on the road that night to see him; however, I was left alone to wait for the man. While waiting, I felt like something bad was going to happen. I saw him and the intention was to talk with him, ask him for some money and go back home because at that point my cousin and I had no food to eat.

I knew something was wrong, but I still got in the car. It drove off and my entire life changed. Everything happened so fast. I was robbed of my innocence. I felt disgusted, I blamed myself.I should have known better. I cried myself to sleep that night. I did not tell anyone about the incident, but I believe Lady Witch assigned monitoring spirits to watch over my life.

However, before that happened, I had a cousin who was a pervert. He would watch me when I was getting dressed or hit me on my bottom when I was washing the dishes in the kitchen. He would also threaten me to go into his room at nights. Coupled with the hard work, those things pushed me to leave that house and when that did not seem forthcoming, I just wanted to die.

While I had not devised a plan to take my life, I was dying on the inside. My innocence was plucked from me, and I was too afraid and ashamed to share same with anyone. However, even in the bad, God orchestrated a plan to interrupt the enemy's scheme. Eventually Lady Witch got wind of what took place and that made her extremely angry with me. I am not sure if it was out of pity or because I did not willingly share with her but one thing for sure the verbal abuse continued until I believed she had enough she told me to leave her home. On hearing that news one would think that I would be sad but I was elated. Elated to leave behind the hurt, brokenness, fears and scars to the possibility of a better life. In spite of the emotional, sexual, psychological and physical abuse I am still alive looking like I have not gone through anything at all, Jesus restores.

CHAPTER 4

MY EXPOSURE TO WITCHCRAFT

REVIVALISM ZION AND POCOMANIA

According to the Jamaica Information Service (JIS) article, "revivalism began in Jamaica between 18610 and 1861 as a part of a religious movement called the Great Revival. It is a combination of elements from African pagan beliefs and Christianity (Mixed) and has several forms, the two major forms being Revival Zion and Pocomania. The rituals involve singing, drumming, dancing, hand clapping, foot-stomping and groaning along with the use of prayers to invite possession. It also includes music and songs from orthodox religion.

During my early teenage years, I was introduced to the revival church by Lady Witch. Of the many occupants of the house, I was the only one who went to the Revival Church with her. Based on the Jamaican culture, revivalism consists of many things such as the use of various coloured candles, baths, oils, bush, chants, and the smoking of the cigar. Additionally, there is the water basin for washing which consists of two machetes and a candle, all of which are used to set the witchcraft altar. Along with the altar, different revival churches carried out baths for individuals; I did not escape the ritual. As I received a bath from the Lady Witch, I remember lighting the candles, setting up the altars in the house and also washing the containers at the end of the ceremony.

One day I was cleaning the cabinet and I saw a lot of small bottles namely, shut up, money, love among others. However, there was something in that pile of bottles that grabbed my attention. Neatly placed among the other bottles was a small bottle in a box marked "Shango" it had a wooden image of an African man.

Needless to say, I was astonished by what I saw, and, out of freight, I hurriedly cleaned the cabinet and left. Some time passed and on my eighteenth birthday I went to a high school to have devotion with my spiritual mother and a pastor.

After the devotional exercise, we were praying on our way to Port Royal, and the pastor started to pray for me. While praying the Holy Spirit moved upon us and the pastor said, "I cut you loose from every Shango spirit." I was so shocked because I did not tell him about what I had seen in the cabinet. Therefore, thoughts began swirling around in my head and I started asking myself a lot of questions. Upon arrival at Port Royal, I told the pastor what he said was true and then I realized that Lady Witch was on assignment for the devil. She was sent to try and abort my God given purpose. After listening, the pastor told me about my mother that she was a prophetess and as her seed I am expected to carry on her legacy; that which she never got to fulfill in her lifetime was now passed onto me, he then prayed for me again. When I arrived home that day, Lady Witch was so mad she cursed me extensively but that was just the beginning of my deliverance. What the pastor told me gave me a newfound hope, the purpose had more meaning, I knew God was still fighting for me.

I remember one night while sitting on the veranda a lady approached my cousin and I. She mentioned, randomly, that she knows a friend who lives overseas who was in the Illuminati or a part of a dark and secret society. She went on to say that the friend had four sons. I was astonished by what I had just heard. However, when she walked away, I heard a still small voice saying, it was her.

I was home on the weekend when I received an image of a can of "black cat powder" from another revivalist. My cousin and I were looking at it when Lady Witch said that she used it to take a man out of jail who molested a young man.

I also remember that there were some people who wanted to do some illegal act and Lady Witch gave them a "bath" and told them to go ahead. Following that incident Lady Witch stayed up all night. When one of my cousins asked her why she was staying up so late she responded, "I am watching the airport to see if it's clear." The bath seemed to work but Lady Witch told them she would not do it again. However, they went the second time without her help and got caught. One day while I was cleaning my cousin's room I climbed on top of the wardrobe where I found one smaller bottle marked confusion. Immediately I knew something was wrong so I called her attention to it but she behaved as if she did not know what it was. She told me to throw away the bottle. However, as I made my way to the garbage intending to break the bottle in the yard the same voice of the Lord said, "no do not do it."

After that incident, my cousins and I were going back to school and Lady Witch bought some oil and instructed us to rub ourselves with it before leaving. My cousin did but I could not bring myself to do it. I could not explain but I just felt something in me saying do not partake of it. Unfortunately, we were not the only ones to share in Lady Witch's rituals. Individuals from all walks of life would come to receive a bath. Additionally, as part of the ritual, she would kill goats and chickens during the holiday season. I actively participated in all the things she would do to perform her works. I did not know those things were wrong. I was truly naïve to the fact, but the Holy Spirit was working behind the scenes, tugging at my heart's door with a gentle reminder that the things Lady Witch practiced were not for me.

CHAPTER 5

DREAMS OF TERROR

One night I dreamt that Lady Witch was in a blue gown standing over me and sprinkling me with liquid from a pan. Right then my spirit got so angry I got up and threw away whatever was in the pan. Next, I saw myself leaving the kitchen then I saw a short black lady standing and on the top of the refrigerator were lots of small bottles. Following those incidents my spirit went back inside my body then I saw myself inside a casket. The casket began breaking and I heard Lady Witch yelling, "how unuh nuh get to bury the casket yet?" "Why is the casket still not buried?" The sun was going down and I awoke from my dream. At that time Lady Witch would only sleep in my room but even amid that reality I still felt a huge blanket covering me and I heard a still small voice saying, "do not be afraid."

Shortly after, I had another dream where someone was telling me that Lady Witch killed the baby. It was so real. When I got up I asked the Lord, "What does this dream mean?" The Lord then revealed to me that it was Lady Witch's first grandson that was sacrificed; the first born for her first son was sacrificed. I am not sure if it was because my stay at the home would soon come to an end but the Lord began revealing a lot of deep spiritual things to me.

THE DREAMS CONTINUED

I was asleep when I saw Lady Witch throwing some brown-coloured mud looking things on me. I began speaking in my heavenly language thereafter the things started falling to the ground. On another occasion I saw Lady Witch's face in a vision; it was covered with makeup. I also saw her cutting red meat in the kitchen sink and the water was so bloody. I was half asleep when Lady Witch walked into the room. With her was a little girl that was staying at the house. As they entered, the girl mentioned that she had a dream that my scalp

29

was peeling off to which Lady Witch said she should stop talking. The next day Lady Witch gave me a cream to rub in my hair and immediately the Holy Spirit said, "do not use it in your hair." Following that incident, a lady, a long-time revivalist, came to the house. We were having breakfast when Lady Witch came into the kitchen and the visitor said, "this young lady is very powerful. Sometime after that day I dreamt that the revivalist who was at the house was climbing on top of me while I slept but I managed to push her off. Thereafter, I would have many encounters, even ones where I felt like I was being suffocated in my sleep.Fortunately the time came and I left Lady Witch's house.

However, even after I left Lady to live with my father the visions still continued. I got visions where Lady Witch was throwing stones and chasing me with a machete to take my life. Additionally, the feeling of being suffocated started getting worse. While I was sleeping, I felt something come over me and tried breaking my neck; it lasted for about a minute. I was just fighting to breathe. Oftentimes I would get panic

30

attacks in my sleep. The feeling of someone coming into my room and trying to suffocate happened for quite some time.

Along with those scary moments, I got a vision that Lady Witch came after me saying "yuh know how long yuh fi dead" "do you know you should have died already?" I never panicked but I got the courage to call a particular name and as that person approached the room, I got the strength to push Lady Witch from where I was staying.

CHAPTER 6
SCHOOL LIFE

I have been through some rough times throughout my school life. I lost my mother in primary school. When I went to live with Lady Witch, I had just completed my GSAT, Grade Six Achievement Test. I began high school the following term. During those years, I was verbally, physically, mentally and emotionally abused. Only through the grace and power of God I was delivered from the strongholds of the enemy. However, the mentioned forms of abuse left me devastated. I suffered from low self-esteem. I hated the way I looked. For some reason I thought my legs were too skinny, my eyes were too small, and my forehead was too big; self-hate overshadowed and engulfed me. I also felt like I was not worthy, a "nobody." I had sleepless nights. Many times, when I went to bed, I thought that I would die from a heart attack. The struggle of a teenage girl trying to find and accept who she was was more than I could bear. With all that I had to endure those around me did not see school as a priority, but I was very persistent. I remember wearing a pair of shoes to school; one foot had such a huge hole at the front that you could see the hole before you saw me; but I wore it anyway. The truth is Lady Witch was more than equipped to buy me a new pair of shoes, but she chose not to. However, amid her nonchalant attitude towards my schooling, I was not daunted. I was eager to learn and to be someone in this life. I was determined to live the life of purpose for which I was destined. I was so resolute that I walked to school almost every day. Lady Witch's house was very far from school, but I would walk and talk with God every morning and that kept me. I did not have any money but thank God for the PROGRAMME OF ADVANCEMENT THROUGH HEALTH AND EDUCATION (PATH) I persevered through the years.

Finally, it was time to sit my Caribbean Secondary Examination Council (CSEC) subjects, but Lady Witch did not pay any money for me to do my examination. Fortunately, my guidance counselor begged her friends on Facebook to donate funds which allowed me to sit my subjects. I felt blessed. I will never forget the reaction re my examination results. Despite the chores, not having any lunch money and enduring the verbal abuse, I ensured that I studied hard. I did ten subjects and got eight. I felt so proud knowing that I had accomplished something.

Now it was time for me to graduate from high school, but Lady Witch did not care about my appearance for that momentous occasion. Therefore, I had the same old uniform, shoes and my hair was a mess. As a result, I went to my father's house and asked one of my cousins to style my hair for the ceremony. After my cousin was finished, I was a little late but I was happy I made it to the graduation. I did not even mention that my friend bought me a pair of shoes, but it was the wrong size. Hence, I was at graduation in a very tight pair of shoes. When I arrived at the ceremony, I saw Lady Witch in the audience well-dressed looking at me. During the service, my name was called for several awards but immediately after that I was told those awards meant nothing. I felt so pressed down and insecure, but I knew deep on the inside that I did my best.

Following my academic recognition Lady Witch did all she could to deny me of every academic opportunity. I was given a half scholarship to do CAPE subjects, but Lady Witch did not allow me to continue my studies. According to her there were lesbians attending the school. Therefore, I was home for a while doing chores. I even went ahead and started applying to different colleges to do social work. In that very season, my mentor, who encouraged me to do social work, sent my application form to The Jamaica Theological Seminary where I went on to study the mentioned course. She applied in 2015 but I did not attend until 2016. I had to differ because of the circumstances at home.

Additionally, the loan company to which I applied did not approve any loan for me so I felt blocked, stuck and purposeless. However, through Christ and the overcoming power invested in me, I left Lady witch's house and started college in 2016. My God is awesome. I finished my Social Work degree in 2021 in fine style. Look at God, my sustainer and my father was always with me.

CHAPTER 7

OVERCOMING ADVERSITY

After all that I went through I gave up. I realized that I was no longer needed because I was defiled. It is amazing how God can work our disappointments for our blessings. I was not seen as being worthy for a sacrifice hence, on several occasions, I was told to leave the house. However, as explained I stayed because I did not want to go back to Payne Land, the inner-city. Therefore, I stayed and endured for a while, but my cup was overflowing. I made up my mind to leave for good, so I started packing my clothes, shoes and books. I had no idea how I was going to leave the house, but I was packing my bags. While I was packing, Lady Witch asked me if I wanted a taxi, deep on the inside I felt like saying no which I did.

Instead, I went and called my spiritual mother; but she asked if I wanted to stay until the next day. However, I felt the urgent need to leave as soon as possible. I then called my father and he said he will speak to someone then call me back. When my father returned the call he mentioned that he knew of a man but he cannot see at night, so he would not be able to come for me. At that moment I did not know what it was, intuition or the prompting of the Holy Spirit, but I knew I could not spend another night in that house. Therefore, I started to pray because I wanted to leave. I remember praying and asking the Lord to break every chain. There was an instant answer to my prayer. That night my father called and said he is coming with my uncle-in-law. When I was getting ready to leave, Lady Witch stood saying, "look what you made me do while shedding a little tear," but I was adamant that I was going to leave. Eventually she told me good luck, in my mind I said, "I do not deal with luck I deal with blessings."

HOME BUT THE WARFARE FOLLOWED

I felt a sense of relief. I started putting my bags on the outside so that it would be easier when the car arrived; I did not want anything to delay the exit. Eventually the vehicle came, I went home that night, and my family welcomed me with open arms.

Days after I arrived home my uncle-in-law called me to say that the night when I was to leave; my father came to his home and was shouting his name. However, it was impossible for him to hear because the neighbour's generator was just too loud. The noise was more than my father's call but, in that moment, he felt the nudge to awake from his sleep and go straight to the door and that was when he saw my father. Thank God I was home, away from Lady Witch, but I still went through a series of warfare. I would have nightmares, dreams of Lady Witch coming after me with stones and machete. Also, I would be attacked in my sleep by cats. At other times I felt the spirit of death in my room, I was just sweating, and I felt like I was going to die.

However, even in the face of death I still believed I was an overcomer. Therefore, I prayed through it all and believed God. Having left Lady Witch, I started attending church and the experience was always awesome. The word would pierce my heart and I would just cry. Countless times I would say to myself now I feel worthy and loved by Jesus Christ. Many times, I would feel his presence holding me at church and at home.

I felt free. I was no longer beside myself. I did not feel like a prisoner to low self-esteem and fear. I learned that I was beautiful and so I fell in love with myself. I no longer saw myself through the eyes of others. I embraced my flaws and what looked like imperfections. I started seeing myself as how God saw me" fearfully and wonderfully made' Psalm 139:14.

I realized that I was unique, and that God made me in that particular manner for a reason and as such the evil words released over my life could not define me. *"Who God bless no man curse," "Greater is He that is in me then he that is in the world."*

Even though those negative words pierced my heart, and I once believed them, the power of God erased those words and set me free.

Today I can say I am not what I went through. I am a victor. I smile today because of the cross of Jesus Christ of Nazareth; He shed His blood for me. I smile today because of His grace and mercy. I am able to love others because of the love Jesus gave and showed me. Now the love of God is so entrenched in my heart. I understand that I was given a sound mind therefore I started to resist the negative things that persons said to me (2 Timothy 1:7).

When I was told that I was ugly, worthless and a bitch, I said mentally, "I am not that and I do not receive it over my life." It is important that we become intentional about the things that we allow to be spoken over our lives. I am who God says I am. I am loved by God. I am the righteousness of God in Christ Jesus. I am redeemed. I am justified. I am sanctified through His blood. I have no fear because I know I can overcome anything with the help of God.

CHAPTER 8
DIALOGUE WITH GOD

Dialoguing with God was my way of coping with all the hurt, trauma and hardships I went through. Owing to the fact that I knew God I wrote to Him and as He spoke to my heart and mind, I made it plain on the papers of my diary. As I reminisce on the journey, I remember clearly one day as my pen hit the paper the tears started to flow. The memories of my life came crashing through, but it was evident the healing process had started.

FEBRUARY 27, 2015

Life is a journey and as I traverse, I have faced a lot of obstacles but nevertheless, said obstacles have made me who I am today. I am bold, ambitious, creative and wise with one hundred percent faith in Jesus Christ. When life gives you hardships, pain, bitterness and unforgiveness, find that inner strength. Pull from your spirit and you will be made whole because the Spirit of

41

God dwells within you. Many individuals do not understand how powerful they are and how they can overcome the hardships, the pain, the bitterness and be whole again.

OCTOBER 12, 2016

An example of the letter I would write to God in my diary. Lord Jesus, I thank You for your love, grace and mercy towards me. It is not the good that I have done but it is your love that has cast out all fears. It is your love that covers a multitude of sins. Lord having You as a father is the best thing. This life is meaningful, but it has a lot of trials and tribulations. However, said trials and tests have built my character thank You Father. Lord when my mother died You were there. You used your servants strongly in my life and I appreciate it a lot.

OCTOBER 14, 2016, 2:10 PM

Lord, I thank You for your love, grace and mercy. On this journey called life, it does not matter where you start but where and how you will finish. I have learnt to live my life according to the Bible, "Basic Information Before Leaving Earth." Lord Jesus I just want to delight myself inYou oh Lord, help me Lord to love You more and more each day.

OCTOBER 14, 2016, 8:30 PM

I love me because, I am confident, no one loves me like I do.

Lord: Do not worry about anything… because I will always be there with you. Do not give up on me because I will not give up on you. I am able. Trust me enough; delight yourself in me because I will honor the desires of your heart according to my word. I honor my word above my very name.

OCTOBER 16, 2016

Thank You Lord that You have allowed me to remember the testimony; it truly blessed my soul... When I think of the goodness of Jesus and all that He has done for me, my soul cries out Hallelujah! Thank You Lord for saving me.

OCTOBER 17,2016

Lord, I thank You for always being there for me in the time when I need You most. Father, I have made mistakes and given into temptation, but those things are not going to stop me from worshiping You. I have fallen many times, but I continue to rise because I know there is hope in You Jesus. So, Lord as I start over I pray that You help me to be who You have called me to be. Lord, please forgive me. Help me to study your word and to retain all that I have studied. Use me according to your will and purpose for my life. You are amazing; there is none like You, Jesus, thank you for life and all that You are doing.

Know that although many negative things were said, and will be said by other people, they do not control your destiny, God does, and He is not like others. He is never changing. He can turn around what the enemy meant for evil to be good in your life. God can turn your scars into stars. Refocus, look in the mirror and encourage yourself as you continue to grow in Christ Jesus.

CHAPTER 9

BROKEN TO BE A BLESSING

I was so broken and undone. I felt like I was nothing.

The abuse, witchcraft and pain had me on a road heading to destruction. I was fighting with the thoughts of suicide. I was overworked and overwhelmed but I have learnt that some of the most beautiful and treasured things in life had to endure a process in order to fulfill their purpose. To be crushed refers to being deformed, pulverized or forced inwards by compression. I was deformed, my spirit was pulverized and my mind crippled. I remember when I was going through my process, I felt beside myself for a longtime. As a result, I felt like I was going to block out. I could not learn or retain anything at all. The mind is very powerful and whatever you desire you can achieve. Even though I was going through the crushing I know I was not cursed. I know that it is the God in me that gave me the courage to fight and persevere. I was not damaged at all, Glory to God.

However, as the olive is crushed to get the precious anointing oil, the grapes to get that sweet aroma and wine, as the material before it turns gold must be crushed and burned by fire, the diamond before it gets that sheen or has that refined look, must go through a process, I too had to be processed. When the different materials went through the different stages it looked as though they were being damaged, but the finished look has many individuals today getting married and using a gold ring or silver as a sign of their love. I have observed that many individuals would take a drink of wine to celebrate life and various milestones. The olive oil is a multipurpose oil, it is used to anoint and bring forth healing, it is used for cooking and many other things. I am sure that when individuals are using these things very few will think about the process it went through to be finalized. At times individuals see the end result of your crushing, some will celebrate with you, some will be astonished but the reality is everything that you went through is producing a champion in you, purpose.

I WAS CRUSHED BUT NOT CURSED

Jesus Himself went through a process of being crucified, to fulfill the purpose for which He came on earth. Everyone has a cross to bear, some trials to fear and some mountains to climb but that does not mean that you are cursed. God allowed the situation to happen so that the purpose that is inside the object can come forth. Likewise, the purpose that is inside you and me shall come forth into greatness.

So, does it mean that the process depicts being flattened or hated? Yes, and it may feel as though you are going to die but it is all in the process. God has a way of putting us through various tests so that we can mature and blossom into the beautiful diamonds and gems that He designed us to be.

One night, through a dream, I was reminded that the road which leads to triumph is never easy, it is narrow, and it requires focus. I saw myself on a huge bike riding on a narrow road, and then I saw a huge truck coming towards me with bright lights. I started panicking because there was nowhere to turn on that narrow road.

I am not sure what happened, but that truck passed without hitting me off the bike and neither of the two vehicles collided; that was God's saving grace. Said grace is achieved through faith. Faith and endurance, though the process may look difficult, are always there to save. I have experienced being saved by God.

Yes, I was flattened. I never knew I would be alive today. I felt like I was going to lose my mind, but it was all in the process. I remember travelling in a bus and I felt everything around me turning; I felt confused. I felt like I wanted to run out of the bus and into the streets. I was overwhelmed by anxiety. I actually had to hold my head, whisper a prayer and then I felt a little better, that part of the process was really scary. I can now share this experience as someone who was mentally challenged or was on the verge of being insane. It took the grace of God and prayers. Today I am smiling, but I have gone through my fair share of trials, behind the perfect picture indeed. I was bruised but not cursed; the pain brought forth purpose. It was through the pain that I realized the depths of Jesus' love for me. Yes, through the pain and the struggle I realized that I am favored by

God. He never allowed the enemy to triumph over me. Yes, I was down for a while, yes, I fell flat on my face but I was victorious in the end.

CHAPTER 10
HOW DID GOD KEEP ME?

It is customary for me to say, "I don't even know how God did it." I believe that God is not slack concerning his promise (2 Peter 3:9). As I reflected on said statement, I am reminded that I am a covenant child and that my mother had asked God for me. Hence, I am in God's care. Even though I went through the rough, God kept me. Today when individuals look at me, they can never tell the type of life I was living or went through because God beautifies me with His salvation and His unconditional love encircles me. Many do not understand but God is real, and He lives within me.

When someone is kept, they are being preserved. I look at the way meat is kept in the refrigerator. The refrigerator is a preserving agent that prevents the meat from spoiling. Additionally, preservatives are placed on various foods to keep them for a very long time and that is the same way God kept me. I recall one night when I was at Lady Witch's house, I was sitting with my cousins outside and a white car pulled up at the gate, then without warning my two cousins were staring down the barrels of guns; I could not see what was happening because of my posture. One of my cousins cried out, 'I ain't scared' and the car drove off. After the car left Lady Witch came and started cursing all of us. However, I was thinking and thanking God for his protection over me and my cousins.

On another occasion God saved my arm from being severely damaged by broken glass. Preservation comes in many forms but some we may not like. While my cousins were allowed to party, I was told to stay inside and if I did not listen, I would be punished. I really wanted to be at the parties but like the meat God was preserving and protecting me. I simply could not understand that God's love was leading my life, so I kept wanting the things that looked glamorous at the time. I wanted to pierce my navel and as a result I went to school and asked one of my friends to take one from the many she had purchased, and she did. I had a desire to please the flesh and was about to make a decision that I would regret so I took home the ring and devised a plan to pierce my navel. I knew I would be punished harshly by Lady Witch, but I did not care. However, once again Jesus who loves me so much intercepted that unhealthy desire that I had in my heart. Nevertheless, I was still not fully surrendered. I still entertained the thought of piercing my navel, but God remained faithful. Therefore, one morning during devotion I heard 2 Corinthians 5: 10-15. "For we must all appear before the judgment seat of Christ, that each one may receive the things done in the body, according to what he has done, whether good or bad. and He died for all, that those who live should live no longer for themselves, but for Him who died for them and rose again. "After reading the scripture I threw down the Bible. Jesus was speaking through the scriptures, and I felt as if the words were lifted off the page and into my face. From that day I was convinced that Jesus is real. The thought of piercing any part of my body simply went. God kept me by protecting me from dangers seen and unseen. God was with me covering me under his mighty hand. I wanted my own way, but purpose must follow the Word of God. There are many things that can happen when you are not in agreement with the things of God. I think that also kept me because I had a relationship with God thus allowing me to understand His desire for my life. Jesus began to show me all I needed to know.

I also learnt that there were consequences for my actions. Said consequences are called opened doors where the enemy can enter and destroy purpose. However, purpose can be kept through the Word of God, reading His words and spending time in your prayer closet talking with Him. After a while I got the boldness to do my devotion in the very house that I was being chastised. I would close the door, pray and sing praises to God. When it became too much for Lady Witch she cursed and told me that she did not like me and that she asked God to take me out of her life. He eventually did and I am grateful. Jesus lives within me. He was there through all my pain, hurt, and struggles. He was there sitting with me watching over me and wiping my tears. Even when the thoughts of suicide came like a river and I wanted to die, God stepped in and reversed all those thoughts. God Kept me.

SELF HATE

Unfortunately, I did not love myself or appreciate the way I looked. I did not like my feet. I struggled with those insecurities throughout my teenage years because of what Lady Witch said about me. I was at a low place, depressed and wished I would just die. Nevertheless, God had a plan, and nothing could stop the plan that He had for me. "For I know the thoughts that I think toward you, says the Lord, thoughts of peace and not of evil, to give you a future and a hope." Jeremiah 29:11 is a scripture that I meditate on because I can relate to Jeremiah's story. He too was a covenant child. Additionally, he had to answer the calling of the Lord to be His mouthpiece.

Now I am able to relate to persons suffering from low self-esteem, depression and those who have been robbed of their innocence. I know what it is like; I can talk to someone who is halting between two opinions. I can minister to someone who is suicidal I remember working at a particular institution and I met a young lady in the hallway. A conversation ensued however as we talked, I observed that she was not looking up but rather on the floor. Then I began encouraging her as the HOLY SPIRIT led me. I told her that she is beautiful, and that bleaching would only damage her skin. I began describing her nose, face and her complexion so she would understand that bleaching her skin was unnecessary. However, I was blown away by her response; there were those who told her the complete opposite of what I was saying to her. Owing to her mindset, it was easy for her to believe the lie. That and others are the simple things that the enemy uses to keep us from rising to our true potential. Psalm 139:14 says, "I will praise You, for I am fearfully and wonderfully made; Marvelous are Your works, and that my soul knows very well." Said scripture helps me to reflect on the fact that God made me special. On the contrary, the devil always makes you feel ugly. He tricks you into thinking there is an issue with the way God made you;

such inferiority is called an identity crisis. It is a prison for many individuals, but I thank God He delivered me and many others who have realized the devil's evil plans for them to hate themselves.

As I said earlier in this chapter, everything that was made had to go through a process. Even the food we eat (ah ah) must go through a process. And yes, I am a foodie.

I remember walking into a coffee shop in Saratoga Corinth New York and I saw nicely wrapped sandwiches; I really wanted to try one. The sandwiches looked good but hearing a friend talking about processed food and its many preservatives caused a blockage. I no longer had a desire to purchase the lovely sandwich. The truth is processed food must be preserved.

That was my life; God preserved me as I went through the process of becoming the woman that He created me to become. I never had the chance to choose my life and that is the beauty of life itself; embracing the challenges, appreciating the struggles and living a life consoled by God. When God has His way in your life it is for Him to be glorified so that others may see His hand on you or the light in you and come to know Him the Only Begotten Son.

CHAPTER 11
JEALOUSY: THE
INEVITABLE

YOUR LIFE IS A THREAT!!

You are alive! You are making strides! You are living a purpose driven life! Everything seems normal but your existence, your achievements have made many very uncomfortable. What does that mean? Should you stop and give into the desires of others? The truth is being great is who God has called you to be. While others remain unhappy or even stop pursuing their dreams just to block you, keep going. David was destined to be the next King, but King Saul could not handle the anointing on his life. Therefore, he left his throne, left ruling a nation just to pursue an innocent man. Although David was only walking in the will of the Lord and doing his best to honour his country, Saul was threatened by the anointing on his life and tried relentlessly to kill him. Jealousy hates the anointing and will lead people to do great evil against you. Saul was the king but as long as David was alive, he was uncomfortable.

Jealousy blinded King Saul. He could not see David as an asset. The man who rid the nation of the Giant Goliath and gave freedom and pride to Israel was now a fugitive because of a jealous king. David only tried to help Saul, but his jealous spirit blocked him. In the same manner Saul was jealous of David's success many have envied and are still envious of what God is doing through me. Jealousy will also cause family members to plot against you. Joseph was not only loved by his father, but he was also a dreamer. He shared his dreams with his brothers and along with conspiring to kill him they sold him into slavery. Be very careful with whom you share your dreams. Dream killers will do anything to discourage, persecute and say ill about you. However, do not be daunted; what Jesus said about you has to be fulfilled. Even though Joseph's brothers sold him into slavery, he was favored by man. Jealousy could not stop God's favour on Joseph's life; what they meant for evil God turned around for his good.

Jealousy was a bullet sent by the enemy to shut down David and Joseph, but God used the enemy's work of art to propel them into their destiny. Like those patriarchs, I have learnt to use jealousy as the springboard to my destiny. Every jealous dagger sent to you must be transformed into steppingstones to burst forth into greatness. Your friends may show signs of jealousy but do not let them halt your God given destiny. Jealousy comes in various shapes and forms. Said emotion is a spirit and can be found in your friends, family, strangers, and colleagues. It is a serious thing when someone is jealous of you. However, I often ask myself, "Why are people always jealous of me." Or why are they so intimidated by me? Many have been so bitter against me that they started spreading lies or gave others the opportunity to have a negative perception of me without knowing who I was. Sigh… it was rough, but that too was a part of the process.

Life has taught me that the enemy does not play fairly; he will literally inject people with the spirit of jealousy so that they will try to derail purpose. Therefore, as was said, those in your immediate environment will start looking at you differently; they will not like the way you dress, speak or your personality as a whole. I am an extrovert, bold, loud and always excited. If I am not excited about something maybe, I am having a bad day. However, I love being the life of any party glory to God. Confident in everything I do. Nevertheless, this personality can be very threatening to others. Hence, people will do and say things with the objective of making me feel less than. Unfortunately, I have encountered two persons in my entire life, which by their very demeanor, made it obvious that they were jealous of me. As a believer, ask God to sharpen your discernment. If you are an unsaved you are at risk of such attacks from the enemy, only God can protect you from the spirit of jealousy.

The Holy Spirit allows the believer to not only discern his or her environment but allows him or her to detect the evil that is being planned in the secret places of the enemy. Additionally, the believer is given strategies to shut down the attacks even before they are formed. However, do not be caught off guard. The enemy may not be the person you expect; said person may just be a very close friend. Once I had a friend, or so I thought, who went at length to make me feel uncomfortable. She highlighted all my flaws and faults in the public space. Mentioned action became a habit and I started feeling a lot of insecurities. Coupled with the evil things that were launched at me, I was experiencing a terrible period that allowed me to be even more broken. The person's actions really affected me but I later learnt that such person was led by the spirit of jealousy. The scriptures warn us to be vigilant. Therefore, let the Holy Spirit heighten your sense of alertness, especially against friends and family members who will never see the good that you have done, but will go above and beyond the call of duty to highlight your flaws. They may say they are only trying to help you to change, but be aware, it may just be an assignment from the enemy to break your spirit.

SIGNS OF THE JEALOUS SPIRIT

Why is she wearing my clothes and imitating me? If you have dreams of people doing said activities, then they are jealous of you. I thank God for His protection. Once God gave me a vision of someone who had the spirit of jealousy towards me; it felt so real I was shocked, but I spoke against the dream taking effect in my life. Shortly after I was conversing with a friend from Canada when she paused during the conversation and said there is someone who is jealous of you. She went on to give me a description of that person and as she spoke, I wanted to cry because it was the same person I saw in my dream wearing my clothing. On another occasion I was doing my examinations and a lady, whose house I was staying, said to me, "there is someone who is jealous of you." Some other things were said about that individual which allowed me to question God because I loved that person dearly. Thankfully God showed me that I ought to pray for that person and against that spirit. I have also learnt that people can be jealous of you just by the way you love and worship God but continue to give Him your best praise and love. Remember:

> People will resent you, keep going.
>
> People will reject you, do not give in.
>
> People will envy you, pray for them.
>
> Take heart *Jesus Christ* lives within you. You are a champion. God made you and me special.

With all that was happening, I had to ask God, "What do I have that allow persons to be jealous of me?" I was not born with any gold spoon in my mouth. I went through so many obstacles, trials and problems. So, what was it? I also asked some of my friends and they would say Deana-Kay you are so confident in everything that you do. However, God said to me when you are going through your trials people are going to be jealous of you. Do not allow that jealous spirit to distract you from where I am taking you. People who are jealous of you cannot stop God from working in your life, it is simply a sign that greatness is within you. Nevertheless, I started to pray about the flaws, insecurities and faults that I thought I had; I gave them all to God. After that full surrender, I learnt to love myself through the divine help of God. Now, I live as the woman of God that He made me to be. I shine without apologizing to anyone who does not like me or the Glory of God on me. Even now this has given me a reason to laugh. I have been through enough to know that God is able.

You may not always understand the fight, but jealousy causes you to give birth to your purpose in this life. How do I know? I did not let what people say about me define who I am in God. The greatest thing is knowing who you are and allowing God to inspire or breathe upon you his breath of life, strength and power. Understand that while it may sound easy, it really is not. Going through the process I cried to God. I vented. I talked to Him about everything. Thankfully, I have now gotten to the point where I have become vulnerable in his presence. I do not hold back anything from Him, I tell Him everything. A broken spirit and contrite heart God will not despise Psalm 51:17.

CONCLUSION

In highlighting all that I have been through as a teenager is to bring awareness to parents and family members. I implore you, ' do not give away your child to anyone.' It does not matter how kind they are to you. We see and know people for years but never underestimate the intentions of their heart. I was abused but my journey from brokenness to being whole positioned me to become a Social Worker. This occupation gives me the autonomy to help other young persons who are having a hard time matriculating through life to become their best self.

Additionally, even though I had the experience of pain, hurt, abuse and trauma, I must say that I have learnt a lot of life lessons. I take life one step at a time by walking in humility and the fear of God. I let go of the past and embrace what is to come. I learn to forgive and love unconditionally. It may have taken me a while for the puzzle to be completed however I am elated that I waited patiently for the time of victory. I write my story to let others know that they are not alone, and no one owns you but God Almighty. As I share my journey, I know it will bless others and help them to overcome by the grace of God.

This is the Lord's doing; it is marvelous in our eyes Psalm 118:23. God is good, I am forever grateful. Behind the perfect picture is a young, brilliant, talented, phenomenal, bold, beautiful, God-fearing young lady who chose to walk with the Lord despite the trials that life throws at her. John 16:33 states, "these things I have spoken unto you, that in me ye might have peace. In the world ye shall have tribulation; but be of good cheer; I have overcome." Jesus overcame so I live everyday fulfilling my purpose. I am an overcomer.

John 16:33 gives me hope knowing that I will have trials, but God will give me peace. He will preserve and be with me in this world of chaos. Through it all maintaining a relationship with God is very important. Witchcraft has no power over you. Greater his He that is in you than he that is in the world. God has given us power to tread upon serpents and scorpions and nothing shall by any means harm us.

Even when everything inside and around you is saying it is a curse, look at life's challenges as a blessing and not an evil. Remember who God blesses no man can curse. In the same manner God kept me, He will keep you.

ABOUT THE AUTHOR

Deana-Kay Thomas is a woman of God who enjoys

singing, dancing, and ministering the Word of God. She
is a social worker by profession, motivational speaker,
worshipper and a youth ambassador who is convinced
that outside of Christ one is not living a potential filled
life. Her mantra is, *"...seek ye first the kingdom of God,
and His righteousness and all other things will be
added unto you." Matthew 6:33*

Deana-Kay Thomas